Blueberry Girl

Blueberry Girl

written by Neil Gaiman

illustrated by Charles Vess

HarperCollinsPublishers

Ladies
of
Light
and
Ladies
of
darkness
and
Ladies
of
never-
you-
mind,

This is a prayer for a blueberry girl.

First, may
you
Ladies
be kind.

Keep her from spindles and sleeps at sixteen,

Let her stay waking and wise.

Nightmares at three or bad husbands at thirty,

These will not trouble her eyes.

Dull days at forty,
    false friends at fifteen—
Let her have
    brave days
    and
    truth,

Let her go places
that we've never been,
trust and
delight
in
her
youth.

Ladies
of
grace
and
ladies
of
favor

and

ladies
of
merciful
night,

This is a prayer
for a blueberry girl.

Grant her your clearness of sight.

Words
can
be
worrisome,
people
complex,

motives
and
manners
unclear,

Grant her the wisdom to choose her path right,

free from unkindness and fear.

Let her tell stories
and dance in the rain,
somersault,
tumble
and run,

Her
Joys
must
be high
as her
sorrows
are
deep.

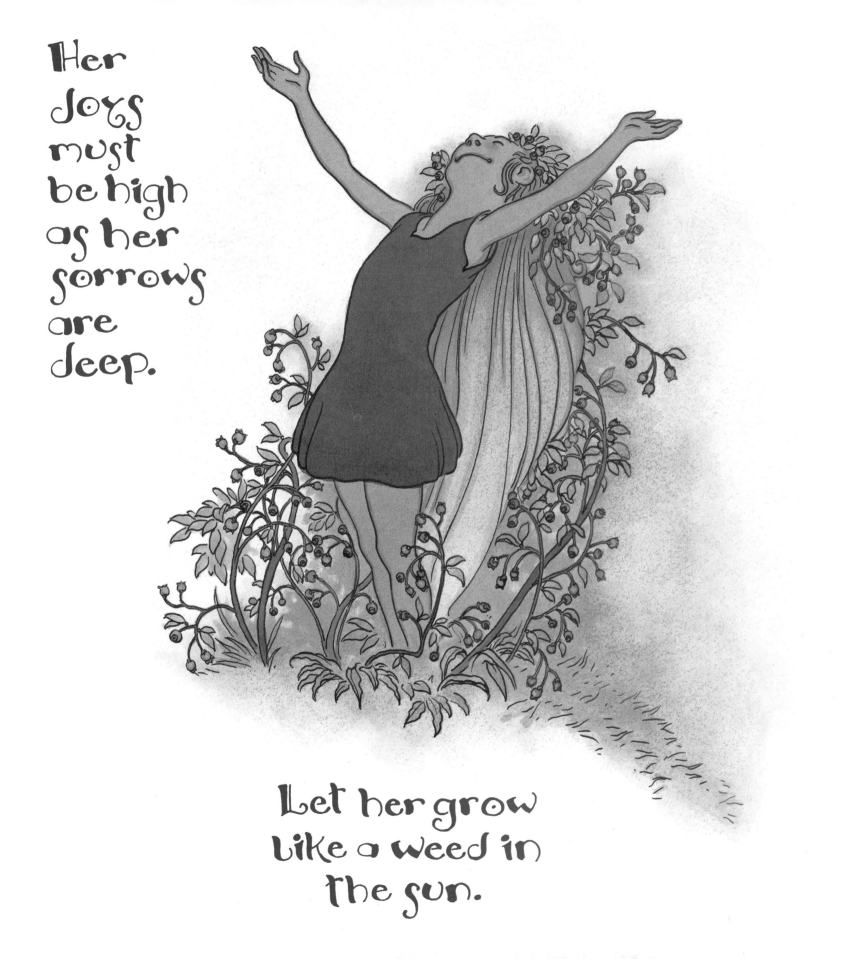

Let her grow
like a weed in
the sun.

Ladies
of
paradox,
Ladies
of
measure,
Ladies
of
shadows
that
fall,

This is a prayer
for a blueberry girl.

Words written clear on a wall.

Help her to help
herself,
help her to
stand,

help her
to lose
and
to find.

Teach her we're only as big as our dreams.

Show her that fortune is blind.

Truth is a thing she must find
for herself,
precious
and
rare
as
a
pearl.

Give her all these and a little bit more:

Gifts for a blueberry girl.

I wrote this for Tori, and for Tash, when she was only a bump and a due date. With love, Neil

This one is for MY MOM, who was always there for me, MY first admirer and critic. All MY love from your son, Charles

Blueberry Girl

Text copyright © 2009 by Neil Gaiman
Illustrations copyright © 2009 by Charles Vess
Manufactured in China.

Library of Congress Cataloging-in-Publication Data is available.
ISBN 978-0-06-083808-9 (trade bdg.) — ISBN 978-0-06-083809-6 (lib. bdg.)

Typography by Charles Vess
1 2 3 4 5 6 7 8 9 10
❖
First Edition